Color My Coral

Heidi Joulios

To my husband, Panos, and children, Apollo and Zoe:
You color my world!
Big love!

To Huckleberry:
Bestest Friends Forever!
Kiss Kiss, Woof Woof!

— H. Joulios

Text and Illustrations copyright © 2013 Heidi Joulios

First Edition

ISBN: 9781936528028

Library of Congress Control Number: 2012933820

Published by
Martin Pearl Publishing
P.O. Box 1441, Dixon, CA 95620

PRINTED IN THE UNITED STATES OF AMERICA

10 9 8 7 6 5 4 3 2 1

Way, way out, in the big bold barrier reef, splendid sea life stirs.
All is serene in the shallow clear waters, until...

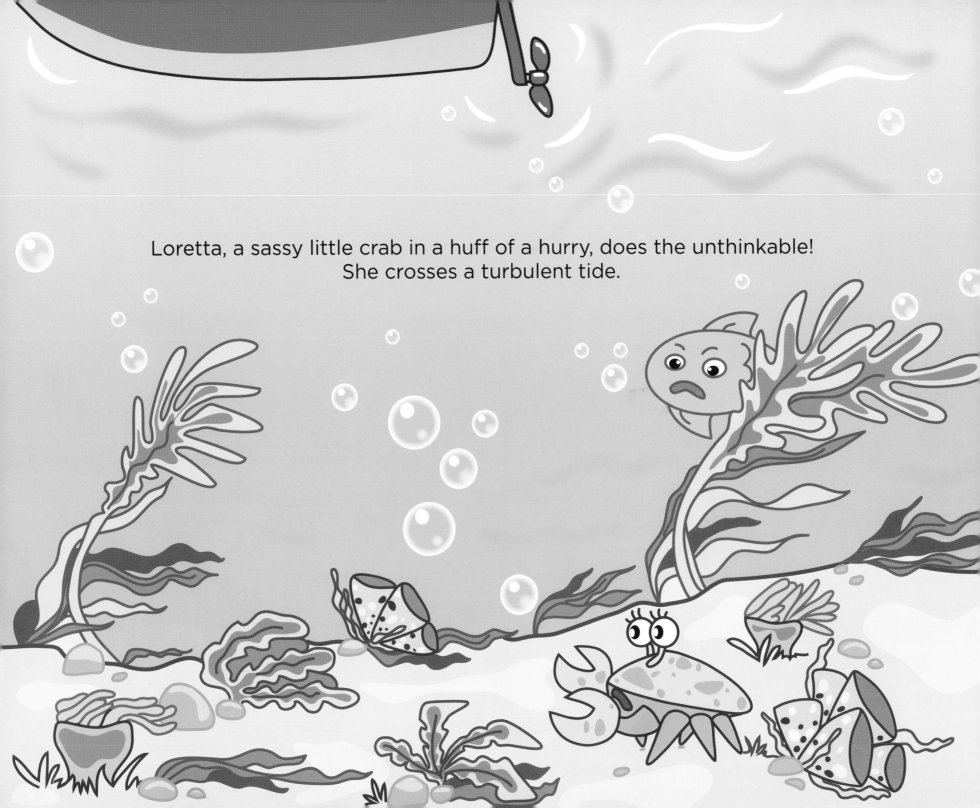

Loretta, a sassy little crab in a huff of a hurry, does the unthinkable!
She crosses a turbulent tide.

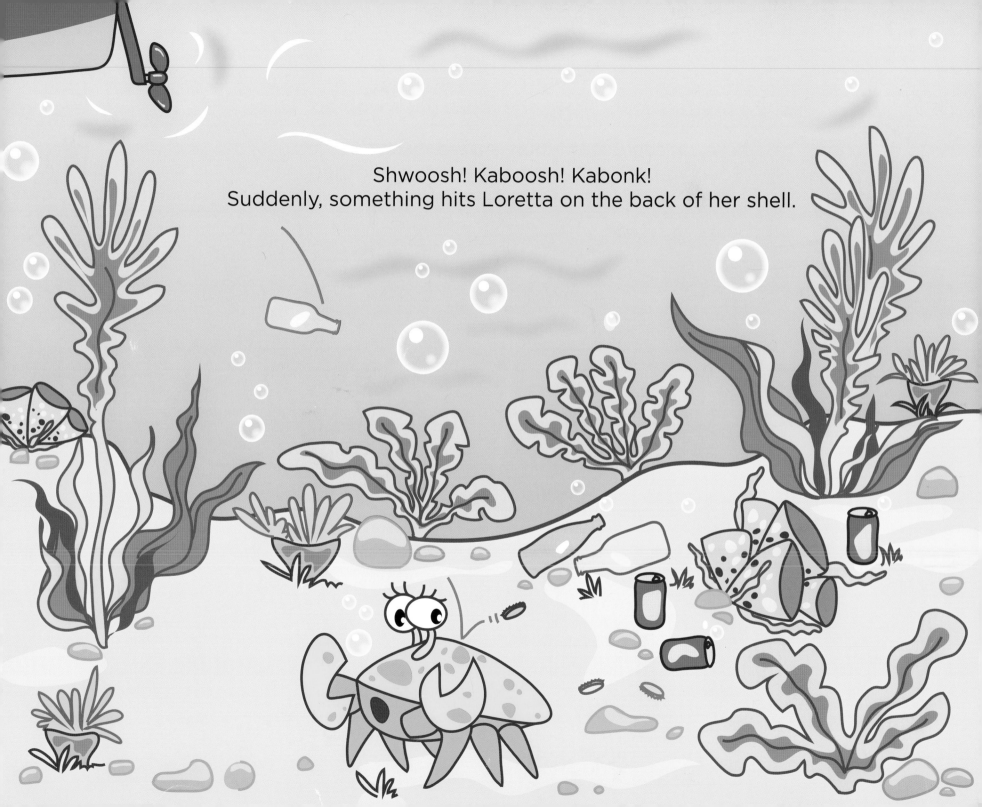

Shwoosh! Kaboosh! Kabonk!
Suddenly, something hits Loretta on the back of her shell.

"Ouch!" Loretta shouts. Then she looks back with an "Oooh!"

There, on the ocean floor, is a wondrous object.
Soon she notices another, and then another.
It's a treasure of a find!

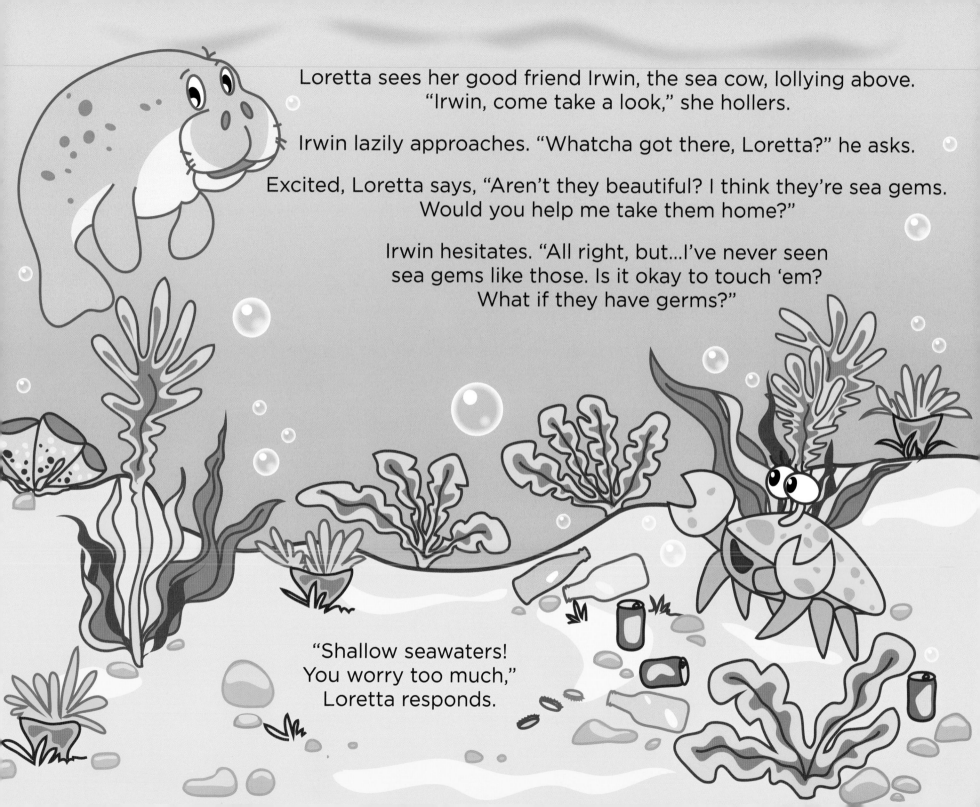

Loretta sees her good friend Irwin, the sea cow, lollying above.
"Irwin, come take a look," she hollers.

Irwin lazily approaches. "Whatcha got there, Loretta?" he asks.

Excited, Loretta says, "Aren't they beautiful? I think they're sea gems.
Would you help me take them home?"

Irwin hesitates. "All right, but...I've never seen
sea gems like those. Is it okay to touch 'em?
What if they have germs?"

"Shallow seawaters!
You worry too much,"
Loretta responds.

Together they carry Loretta's treasures, carefully making their way through the seaweedy waters and the sandy seabed to her home in the coral reef.

Clicking her claws with excitement,
Loretta decorates the front of her house,
placing the new objects all around the reef.
Even the coral polyps are charmed
by the unusual objects.

"We are sure to catch the neighbors' attention," pipes in a polyp.

"I can't wait for the compliments," Loretta proudly says.

That night, an exhausted Loretta crawls into bed.

Thinking about her marvelous day, she sighs a happy sigh.

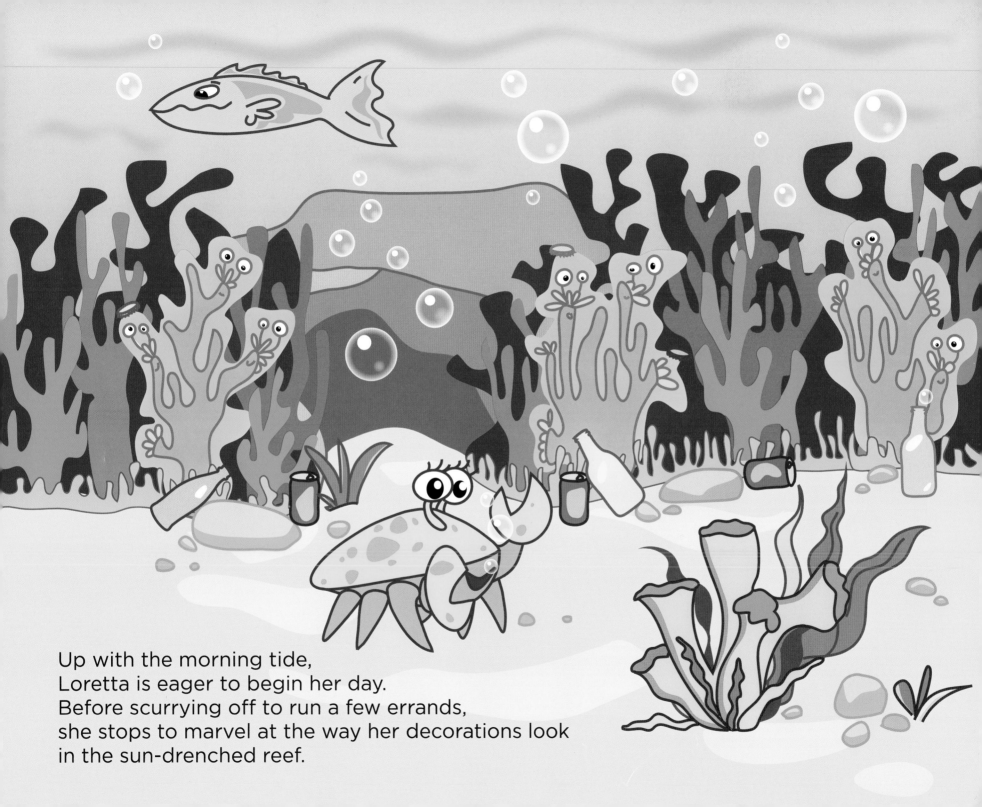

Up with the morning tide,
Loretta is eager to begin her day.
Before scurrying off to run a few errands,
she stops to marvel at the way her decorations look
in the sun-drenched reef.

Word travels fast! Loretta is stopped by a wave of chatter at the Corner Cove.

"Wowza! Everyone is talking about your place, Loretta," says her good friend, Betty, the lobster.

Oliver, the sea slug, adds, "What a wonderful display of extraordinary objects! Your house looks amazing, simply amazing!"

Puffed Up Patty remarks, "Well, your house certainly stands out in the neighborhood."

Loretta basks in the attention as the wave of chatter continues.

Making her way through an almost perfect day, Loretta returns home to a startling find. The coral is losing its color and turning white!

"Yikes! What's going on?" Loretta yells.

Suddenly, she hears a coral polyp cry, "I don't feel good."

"Well, your color's not good!" Loretta replies.
"I'll get Arty. He'll know how to fix your color."

Just a wave and a half away,
Loretta finds Arty in his grotto.

With a mouth full of bubbles, she blurts,
"I need your help! I have color trouble!
Hurry! Grab your inks and brushes!"

As they approach Loretta's house, Arty is stunned by what he sees.
"Crazy clams! The coral is losing its color!" he shouts.

"Hush, I don't want the neighbors to know," Loretta whispers.
"Tell me, can you color my coral?"

Arty confidently answers, "Of course I can! Color is my specialty!"

To create the perfect shade of orange,
Arty mixes a splash of yellow
and a dash of red.

With a stir, a dip, and a dabble,
he carefully paints over
the fading coral.

Bursting with excitement,
Loretta cheers, "You did it!
You colored my coral!"

Arty simply smiles with delight.

The very next morning, Betty arrives at Loretta's door with alarming news. "The polyps are coughing, sniffling, and sneezing," she cries.

Loretta looks outside. Surprisingly, she finds...the coral is fading! Again!

"Drats! This is dreadful!
Get the doctor, Betty!" Loretta yells.

Dr. Eel receives Betty's frantic call for help over the tele-shell.

"The polyps are sick! Come quick!" she pleads.

Wiggling swiftly, Dr. Eel makes his way to Loretta's house.
The sight is astonishing! He has never seen a reef look so pale.
Dr. Eel checks the coral polyps and listens carefully to their symptoms.

"Ahhhh-*chewie!* Sniff, sniff, *sneezle!* Hack, hack, *honk!*"

The sickly sounds catch the neighbors' attention and a crowd begins to gather in the reef.

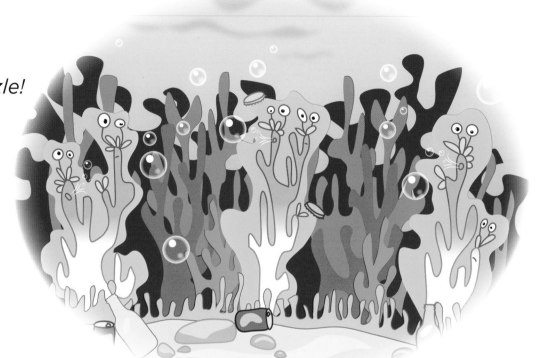

Irwin pokes his pudgy nose in to ask, "What's goin' on?"

"Shhh! The doctor is examining the reef," Loretta says.

The water becomes strangely quiet just before Dr. Eel announces, "It's a germ! There is a harmful germ in the reef! That's why the polyps are so sick!"

The crowd gasps!

"This is shocking news! How did this happen?" Oliver asks.

Puffed Up Patty answers abruptly, "Well, I think it's all that strange stuff Loretta put around her house."

Irwin remarks, "I knew those things had germs!"

Loretta confesses, "I didn't know the polyps would get sick!
I didn't know these sea gems had germs!"

"Gems?" Puffed Up Patty interrupts. "They don't look like any sea gems I have ever seen.
They look like garbage!"

The chatter continues, but this time there is a wave of concern.

"Great Groupers! If the germs spread to the rest of the reef...
it would be a color catastrophe!" Arty declares.

"Let's not panic!" Dr. Eel announces.
"The coral polyps were healthy without these things.
It's an easy remedy. Let's remove them."

They all agree.

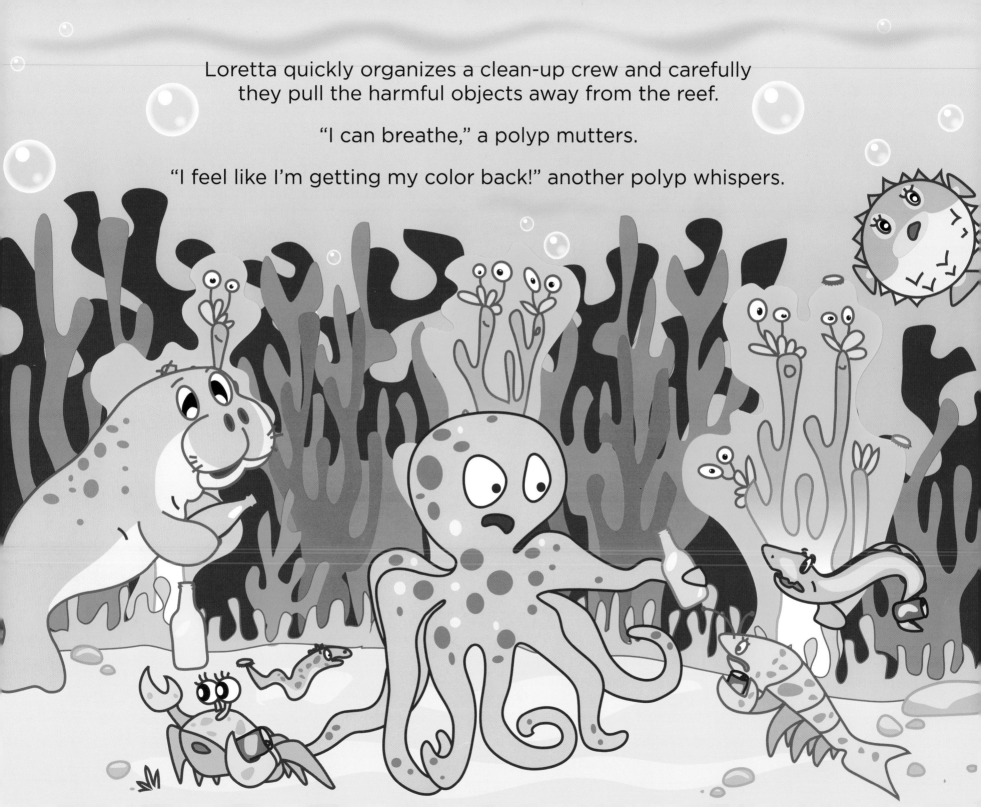

Loretta quickly organizes a clean-up crew and carefully they pull the harmful objects away from the reef.

"I can breathe," a polyp mutters.

"I feel like I'm getting my color back!" another polyp whispers.

The job to rid the reef of the germy garbage continues.

Puffed Up Patty asks, "Where do we dump this junk?"

"I suggest we get it out of the water before anyone else gets sick!" Dr. Eel replies.

The crew is quick to follow Dr. Eel's advice. They journey onward, carrying the items across the ocean floor, slowly making their way to shallow waters.

Suddenly, the clean-up crew is swept up by a big wave.

Away they go! *"Woo hoo!"* the group shouts, riding the wave up to the shore.

Quickly they toss the garbage onto the beach, leaving it in one big heap.

As the crew rolls back into the sea, they sigh with relief.

"Whoopie! We are germ free!" Irwin yells.

Huddled together, the crew takes a peek to see the garbage they left behind on the beach.

Suddenly, Betty cries, "Oh, no! What did we do? What if the land gets sick and loses its color, too?"

Puffed Up Patty remarks, "Well, that's not *our* problem."

"The land won't get sick," Dr. Eel declares. "Look!"

The group sees kids picking up all the garbage on the beach and putting it into a bag.

"Jumpin' Jellyfish!" Loretta shouts. "The land has a clean-up crew, too!"

"What a splendid sight! Simply splendid!" Oliver adds.

Gazing at the land with all of its beautiful color gives everyone hope.
Happily, the crew heads for home in the colorful coral reef.
Once again, all is serene in the shallow, clear waters.

Hey kids!

Some Coral Facts:

Did you know that corals found in our oceans are living creatures? In fact, corals are built by teeny tiny sea animals called **"polyps."** Colonies of coral can create big colorful reefs. But, did you know that coral can also *lose* its color? **It's true!** When coral loses its color, it's called **"coral bleaching."**

If coral becomes damaged, stressed, or catches a virus (like when you catch a cold), it will lose its color. Pollution is stressful to coral reefs and can cause coral bleaching.

Some activities we do throughout the day can create **pollution**, which harms the earth and its oceans. Pollution, from plastic wrappers, water bottles, garbage and chemicals, finds its way into the ground, air, and waterways, and can be harmful to all living things. We can help to keep our coral reefs healthy and colorful if we try not to pollute.

Just think...by setting out to help teeny tiny sea animals, we make a great big difference on Earth.

Healthy Coral

Wowza!

Bleached Coral